Hardwick House

Purdey's Pasture

River Noodle

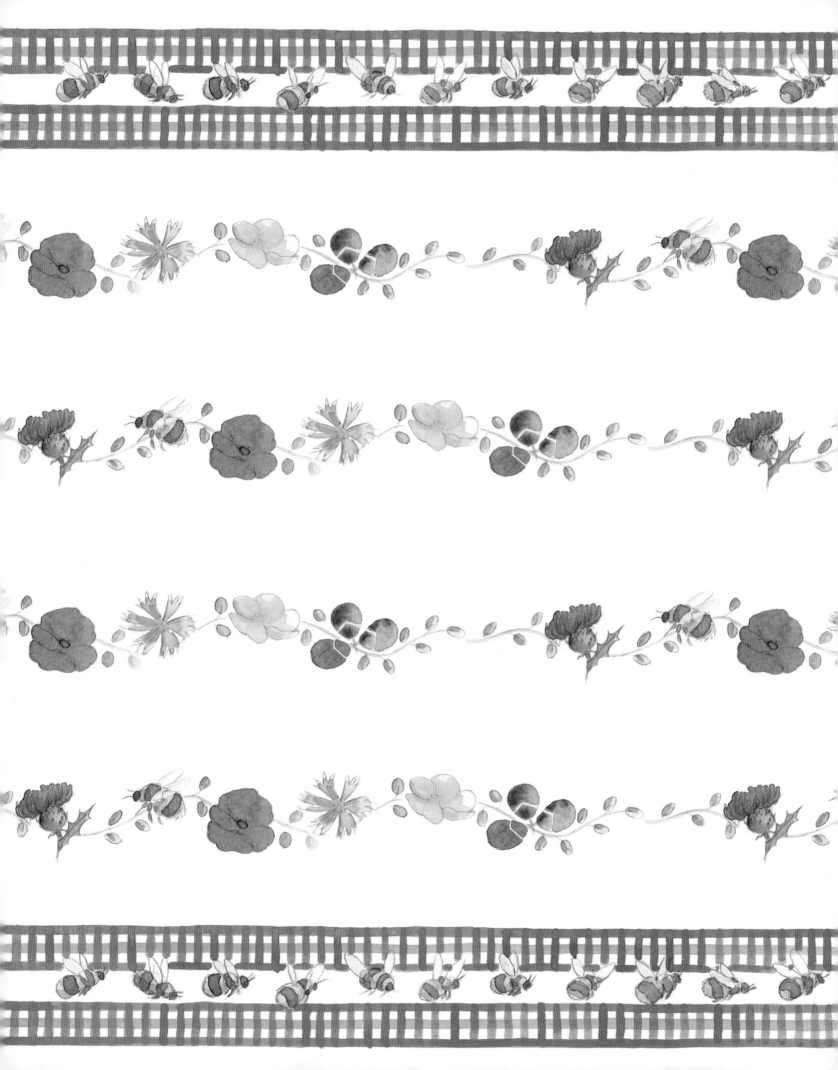

For P. J.—the true inspiration for Little Red
—S. F.

For Iris and Robert
with love
—S. W.

SIMON & SCHUSTER
BOOKS FOR YOUNG READERS
An imprint of Simon & Schuster
Children's Publishing Division
1230 Avenue of the Americas,
New York, New York 10020
Text copyright © 2006 by Sarah Ferguson,
The Duchess of York
Illustrations copyright © 2006 by Sam Williams
All rights reserved, including the right of reproduction in whole or in part in any form.
SIMON & SCHUSTER BOOKS FOR YOUNG READERS is a trademark of Simon & Schuster, Inc.
LITTLE RED is a trademark of Sarah Ferguson, The Duchess of York, and is used under license.
Book design by David Bennett
The text for this book is set in Goudy.
The illustrations for this book are rendered in soft pencil and watercolor on Arches paper.
Manufactured in China
2 4 6 8 10 9 7 5 3 1
Library of Congress Cataloging-in-Publication Data
York, Sarah Ferguson, Duchess of, 1959-
Little Red's summer adventure / Sarah Ferguson, the Duchess of York ;
illustrated by Sam Williams.— 1st ed.
p. cm.
Summary: Little Red saves the River Noodle Boating Bonanza from a pesky magpie.
ISBN-13: 978-0-689-85562-7
ISBN-10: 0-689-85562-1 (hardcover)
[1. Dolls—Fiction. 2. Boats—Fiction. 3. Magpies—Fiction.] I. Williams, Sam, 1955- ill. II. Title.
PZ7.Y823Ll 2006
[E]—dc22
2004025037

Little Red's
Summer Adventure

Sarah Ferguson
The Duchess of York

Illustrated by
Sam Williams

Simon & Schuster Books for Young Readers
New York   London   Toronto   Sydney

Name: _____

Color By Number

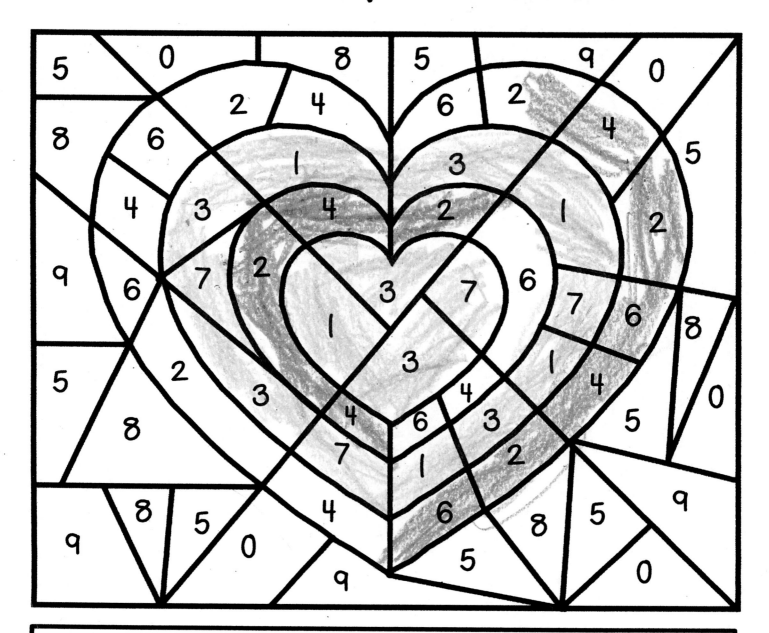

Key:
Color Pink: 1, 3, and 7
Color Purple: 2, 4, and 6
Color Red: 5, 8, 9, and 0

It was a sizzling hot summer's day at Buttercup Cottage. Butterflies fluttered and bees buzzed busily amongst the daisies and the clover. Gino ran between Little Red and Little Blue, wagging his tail as usual and barking happily.

"I'm just so excited!" cried Little Blue as he jumped from foot to foot. "The River Noodle Boating Bonanza is always so much fun. What a buzz of a day!"

Roany stood by the wonky wooden wagon. "Do we have to go?" she asked grumpily. "I always end up giving pony rides and it's just too hot! I want to stay in the shade."

"Giddyup!" said Little Red cheerfully. "You know how much everyone loves your rides—you're the star attraction."

She plopped a floppy hat on Roany's head. "This will keep you cool!" she said.

Roany smiled; she was secretly pleased about being so popular.

"All right then," she snorted, "so long as I have an enormous bucket of iced carrot juice to drink."

They hadn't gone far when, all of a sudden, a great pigeon crashed and skidded onto the roof of the wonky wooden wagon. "I really must practice my landings."

"Blakesley Bill!" guffawed Roany, happy to see her old friend. "I knew you'd come."

"Wouldn't miss the River Noodle Boating Bonanza for the world," chuckled Blakesley Bill. "What's the prize for the winning boat this year?"

"A chance to turn the magic key on the wonky wooden wagon . . . ," began Little Red.

"So that it turns into a super summer surprise," interrupted Little Blue, jumping up and down.

Just then the wonky wooden wagon trundled around a bend in the lane and the River Noodle came into view.

And what an amazing sight it was!

"Jumping jelly beans!" exclaimed Little Blue as he looked on in awe.

Little Red stared, tongue-tied—the river had never looked so beautiful.

Purdey pranced busily by the boathouse.

"I've made heaps of juicy Jell-O, marvelous marshmallow meringues, and whipped watermelon ice cream," she said proudly. "I just need some help to push the Jelly Boat into the water—it's going to be a floating, boating sweetie bar!"

"Scrumtilicious!" said Little Blue, licking his lips.

Little Red delved into a box of paper hats and started to hand the hats out to all of the contestants. Then she called for everyone to climb aboard their boats.

"I love the badgers' painted wheelbarrow, and the squirrels' watering can is beautifully polished," she whispered to Bear, "but the robins look so pretty in their little teacup and don't the rabbits look dandy in their old boot too."

"What do you think of our Hardwick House gravy boat?" called Mole.

"Surely the prize is ours!" added Vole.

"Let's just wait and see!" replied Little Red kindly. "Oh look, the field mice have really gone to town with their cheese board—what a clever idea. And, my goodness, a boat full of holes!" giggled Little Red. "How are you going to keep afloat?"

"Ladles!" spluttered Duck and Goose, baling out frantically.

"How on earth are you going to decide who wins?" puzzled Little Blue.

"I'll have a careful think while we go over to see how Roany's getting on," replied Little Red.

"Roll up! Roll up!" chirped Blakesley Bill, helping a group of frogs onto Roany's back.

"Laughing leapfrogs!" croaked the littlest frog. "I could never jump this high. I can even see Hardwick House."

"Is everything okay?" asked Little Red.

"I suppose so," muttered Roany, "but surely it must be time for a break."

Little Red carried over a bucket of ice-cold carrot juice.

"Have a good, long sip and a quick rest while I announce the Boating Bonanza winners," she said as she nuzzled Roany's muzzle.

Little Blue honked his horn loudly and at once there was a hush. The only sound came from the whispering waters of the River Noodle.

"This year the boats are more spectacular than ever!" announced Little Red. "But there has to be a winner, and I've decided that the prize should go to . . . the rabbits!"

"Hurrah, hooray, whoopee!" Everyone cheered and clapped. Little Red carried the baby rabbits up the ladder so that they could scamper onto the roof.

But, just as they were about to turn the key, a magpie swooped down and snatched it clean away.

"Oh, you naughty, nasty nuisance!" exclaimed Little Red as the magpie soared into the sky.

But the key was too heavy for the magpie and it fell into the River Noodle with a huge SPLOSH!

"Coconut cupcakes!" shrieked Little Blue as he ran to the water's edge. "We'll never find the key now!"

At that moment, Mr. Ron Bow popped his head out of the water. "Hello, everybody!" he said. "You'll never guess what just happened. There I was, swimming along, minding my own business, when—out of nowhere—an enormous key bopped me on the end of the nose!"

"I'm so sorry," said Little Red. "It's the key to our wonky wooden wagon, but a very naughty magpie just tried to steal it. Is there any chance you could get it for us?"

"Okay, lass, I'll do my best!" said Mr. Ron Bow, giving a quick salute and diving beneath the surface. Moments later he popped up again.

"Terribly sorry, my dear," he puffed. "What did you just ask me to do? You know us trout. Memories like goldfish!"

"The key . . . ," began Little Red.

"Of course. Silly me!" apologized the trout. "Won't be a tick!" And with that he splashed back into the river. And then back up again!

"I hate to be a nuisance," he spluttered, "but if you could just remind me . . ."

"Oh dear," said Little Red. "I think we're going to need someone else's help here!"

Little Red, always prepared with her sack of smiles, reached into it and took out her magic bubble blower. She began to blow tiny rainbow-colored bubbles all over Gino's fur.

All of a sudden with a fizz, pop, flash, bang, wallop, Gino turned into a dogfish!

In one graceful movement he dived into the River Noodle.

Down, down, down he doggy-paddled. Past forgetful Mr. Ron Bow. Even past a winking, whiskery catfish. Gino was desperate to give chase, but he knew he was on a very important mission so he kept on swimming.

Suddenly he saw the golden magic key, half buried in the riverbed. Gino flicked it free with his tail.

"Bravo!" shouted the crayfish, who were watching in amazement.

With a triumphant splash, Gino leapt out of the water, dropping the key at Little Red's feet.

"Well, blow me down with a feather!" exclaimed Blakesley Bill.

"Fishtastic!" cried Little Blue as he cartwheeled round in circles.

Gino shook himself dry and back into his doggy shape.

"Woof, woof!" he barked. He was happy to have a tail to wag again.

"Gino, you're a hero!" cheered Little Red, and she kissed his head.

"And now," she said to everyone, "the little rabbits shall turn the magic key on the wonky wooden wagon."

"I'll circle overhead to make sure that pesky magpie doesn't come back," said Blakesley Bill as he prepared for takeoff.

"Let the surprise now start before our eyes!" announced Little Red.

With a puff of smoke . . . a whiz and a whirl . . . a clutter and a clatter . . . and a flicker of tiny fairy lights . . .

. . . the wagon turned into the most beautiful carousel.

Each one of the brightly painted horses looked just like Roany!

"Splendiferous!" cried Little Blue.

"WOW!" everyone gasped. As they climbed onto the little horses, the sun was beginning to set and the carousel spun round and round. The River Noodle looked even more magical than ever.

"Thank you, everyone, for such a wonderful day," said Little Red. "I think this has been the best Boating Bonanza ever!"

The Village

Lily Pad Pond

Buttercup Cottage